FSC
www.fsc.org
MIX
Papier aus verantwortungsvollen Quellen
Paper from responsible sources
FSC® C105338

Bibliografische Information der Deutschen Nationalbibliothek: Die Deutsche Nationalbibliothek verzeichnet diese Publikation in der Deutschen Nationalbibliografie; detaillierte bibliografische Daten sind im Internet über dnb.dnb.de abrufbar.

Verlag: BoD · Books on Demand GmbH, In de Tarpen 42, 22848 Norderstedt, bod@bod.de
Druck: Libri Plureos GmbH, Friedensallee 273, 22763 Hamburg

Sex on Sagea

Roman, an inconspicuous student with a passion for online games, stumbles across a new type of computer game one day. What he doesn't suspect at the time is that this game will revolutionize his sex life in a way he could never have imagined in his wildest dreams.

In „Sex on Sagea", Roman immerses himself in a virtual world full of sensual adventures and erotic encounters. Every quest is a new challenge, every encounter a chance to improve his skills and live out his most secret fantasies.

With each page, a world of passion and desire unfolds as Roman learns to overcome his fears and explore his sexual desires. From shy beginnings to daring escapades, these short stories take the reader on a journey through Roman's erotic transformation.

„Sex on Sagea" is more than just a book - it is a sensual experience that blurs the boundaries between reality and fantasy.

Table of contents

A personal note:
The translation of this book 6
Start area 8
The journey to Kavna 38

ISBN: 978-3-7693-1332-1

Translation:

The translation of this book from the original german into english was done in the first instance by artificial intelligence (AI) and then corrected by me.

Since I am not a native english speaker, the text may contain errors. Please excuse this.

A personal note: The translation of this book

Until that point, readers of my story only had the opportunity to get the german version of the book to read it. Therefore, I had been thinking for some time about having the book translated into other languages, at least into english to start with.

I am not a native english Speaker. Admittedly, I am able to speak english to make myself understood in foreign countries – where english is understood – but I knew that this alone is not enough to translate an entire book into this language... I didn't have the money for a professional translation agency, so I put this idea aside. It wasn't realizable at the moment.

But then came artificial intelligence:

After I heard about artificial intelligence and tried some things with it, I noticed that the results that this new technology produced were getting better and better, so after a year I gave the project of „Book translation into english" another chance. I first asked the artificial intelligence to roughly translate the book. Then I made corrections and other improvements myself.

The result is this book now.

I hope that you, dear readers, enjoy it and forgive any translation errors.

And now the story.

Start area

Now I'm excited! From what the salesman said, it must be overwhelming. I'm waiting for something to happen. Some feeling, an image, a sound ...

Slowly a picture emerges. Water ... It reaches as far as my eyes can see.

The sound of the sea ... The typical clapping of water against a beach. I feel sand under my feet ... warmth on my skin ...

It feels like ... summer!

„Wow..!“, I hear myself say.

The salesman said that the experience was as realistic as if you were actually there, but I never expected to feel it with all my senses!

I can even smell the salty sea air! It feels like being on vacation, it smells so wonderful. I take a deep breath and enjoy ...

But why am I naked? The seller didn't say anything about that ...

I also can't imagine that this could be intentional. Why would you send players into their first adventure completely naked? That makes no sense!

As I look down at myself, I see my virtual body and am once again very impressed. It looks exactly like my body in the real world. Even the hair on my legs, my penis, the slight tummy bulge and many other little things match.

„Unbelievable!“

As I pronounce the words, I realize that my voice is also perfectly pitched.

I look around me. In front of me is the sea, below me the sandy beach and behind me, a few meters away, a small house that looks like a bar.

I wonder what drinking feels like in this game?

As I approach the bar, I see a blonde lady with long curly hair standing at the bar preparing something. So that she doesn't see that I'm naked, I quickly walk to the bar behind her and, once there, use the counter as a privacy protection.

„Hello!“, I try to attract her attention, and as if she had just been waiting for me to call her, she turns around and smiles at me.

„Hello, what can I do for you?“

She looks me up and down with a mischievous grin. But my body is covered by the counter from the tummy down.

„Hello“, I repeat again. „What is there to drink here and how much does it cost?“

As I ask the question, I remember that I have just arrived here, naked and therefore I have no money with me.

She lists a few alcoholic cocktails that you can usually also get at a bar in the real world. But I’m not in the mood for that right now, so I ask her for a nonalcoholic drink and when she has taken the order, I tell her that I don’t have any money with me.

„My handsome one! Here on the island, you pay with gold, silver and bronze coins. Or, if you prefer, with your seed.“

With my seed?

The seller said that any man can have sex with any woman in this game and that the sex feels real. As if you were having real sex right now.

Nevertheless, I want to know more and ask.

„So, I’m going to sleep with you and pay for my drink that way?“

„You can also sleep with one of the other beautiful women here if you want. Shall I introduce them to you?“

„No, I'm completely satisfied with you! Make me a good cocktail, please. One that you would drink yourself. But without alcohol, please!"

„All right! Non-alcoholic, coming right up!"

When she has finished her work, she comes back to me and puts the cocktail on the bar.

„Here you go, enjoy it!"

I pull on the straw and let the first sip work its magic on my tongue.

The fact that I can taste the cocktail is impressive, but I'm even more impressed by the beauty of the bartender in front of me in her mini bikini.

My words seem to make her happy. She leans towards me as far as the counter will allow it and licks my lips tenderly.

„Mmm, that's right! I did really well with this one today!"

Now she walks around the counter. She emphasizes the movement of her hips and when she reaches me, she takes my hands in hers so that I can no longer protect my pubic area. I sit down on the bar stool next to me. She slowly guides my hands up her sides to her bikini top, and as she does so, she caresses my lips with her tongue and carefully works her way further into my mouth.

With my hands she now slips her bikini top off her breasts, which tempts me to caress them.

I now want to know what the rest of her body feels like, so my hands slowly move down and touch every millimeter of her. When I reach her belly, she pulls it in slightly. She must be a little ticklish in this area.

Now I move my hands further down over her hips and notice that she no longer wears her bikini panties. When did she take it off?

I stroke the round shape of her bottom. She cradles it in my hands and I pull it towards me until it comes to rest on my lap, feeling my penis penetrate her. I let out a deep „Ahh...“. Her legs wedge to the right and left of me and I can feel that I won’t need much longer to reach orgasm.

I want to move my penis inside her, but it’s not that easy sitting on the bar stool. To my delight, she seems to take over. She gyrates her pelvis in smaller and larger movements, sometimes slower and sometimes faster. As she breathes, she lets out a sensual moan again and again, which makes me desire her body more and more.

She now bends her upper body back into a hollow back while moving her pelvis quickly, holds on to the counter and puts her head back. Her long wavy hair falls back and she shows me her full breasts and slender neck.

My hands move up now. Over her waist, to her tummy, further over her ribs and to her breasts, which I hold tightly.

I kiss her neck fervently as I feel the orgasm and let all the energy escape through my penis.

When the waves of discharge are almost over, I thrust my hips against hers a few more times. She supports me by skillfully completing the movement and as I fall forward into her arms, completely satisfied, I laugh out loud with excitement.

She looks deep into my eyes and whispers in my ear:

„Congratulations on completing your first challenge!“

She climbs off me. My penis, which is still a little stiff, slips out of her. She moves away from me, puts on her bikini and when she gets behind the bar she grins at me like someone who has just had fantastic sex.

„Hey, handsome! This is your reward!“

She is holding an item of clothing in her hand, which she passes to me over the counter. I take it and see that it’s a pair of shorts made of thin fabric, similar to boxer shorts.

That makes me laugh ... This is what I've been wishing for ever since I realized I was naked. I slip into it immediately and enjoy the fabric against my skin ...

What is still missing is something to cover the upper body.

I'm getting ready to leave the bar when the bartender points to an envelope lying on the counter in front of me.

„By the way, this message is for you!"

Surprised that there is suddenly something for me at the counter, I pick it up. It's made of yellowed paper and looks old-fashioned. Two flattened drops of red sealing wax, each stamped with the game's logo, seal it.

I open the envelope and break the seal. Inside is a folded, yellowed piece of paper. I unfold it and try to read it. The words are written in barely legible cursive letters, but I still manage to decipher the letter somehow:

Hello Roman!

Congratulations on completing your first challenge!

As you have already noticed, having realistic sex is an important part of the game.

How does it work?
** For every orgasm you have while playing the game, you will receive a sum of money in your account.*
** If you send your semen to us, we will analyze it and add a larger or smaller bonus to your account, depending on the quality of the semen, of course.*
** You will receive a further bonus as soon as we have been able to use the seed profitably.*

A few tips:
1. Say: „Inventory" if you want to see what you are carrying.
2. If you want to leave the game, let the game know by saying „Leave game".

Now have fun on Sagea!
Your Sex on Sagea team.

I put the letter in the envelope and put it back on the counter.

So the salesman was serious when he said to me:

„You could earn a lot of money in this game without having to do much..."

Of course, what people doesn't want to have a good orgasm from time to time, preferably with a partner they like! If it feels so realistic in the game, you might not need a real person for it in the future and even earn a few euros alongside. And all this without having to worry about sexually transmitted diseases or pregnancy! That's brilliant.

Above all, it's ideal for people like me. People who are afraid of talking to real people on first sight.

And who knows what the future holds: If I have sex with other players here in the game, we could also meet up in real life.

But now I want to try out the inventory.

I say, „Inventory.“

A wooden chest appears on the sand next to me.

I leave my seat at the bar and want to open it, but when I touch it, the lid pops open a crack of its own accord. I tilt it all the way back and look inside the chest. Inside is what looks like an antique cash box. I take it out and open it. Inside is a golden coin.

A golden coin ... Is this the starting capital?

And what is it worth here in the game?

I put the coin back, close the chest and watch to my surprise as it disappears. It looks like it disappears into thin air ... Interesting!

Now I let my gaze wander across the landscape to find out where to go next. I spot a high fence in some distance away that looks like it has a gate right in my field of vision. I go there, open the fence gate and step out of the beach property.

Now the ground no longer feels so familiar to my feet, like a sandy beach and a vacation, but like cold, flattened earth.

To my left and right, a path is made of the same trampled earth and seems to lead out of the city. In front of me, a path, also of the tramped earth, leads between two rows of wooden houses to a fountain some distance away. Everything here has a medieval charm. It could really have looked like this back then.

Next, I want to read the game instructions to find out what the rules are for sending in the semen. It's in the game box under my bed and that means I have to log out.

But how do I do that?

I remember the message from the bar in the beach area and say in clear tone: „Leave game!“

A second later, a voice says: „Logging out.“

The image before my eyes goes black and the background noises disappear. Shortly afterwards, I no longer feel like I'm standing on cold ground with my bare feet, but laying on something soft and cozy.

I open my eyes. I'm lying in bed exactly as I was before I started the game, looking up at the ceiling of my small student room. I can clearly feel the tight data hood that the game told me to put on before starting the game.

I sit up, peel the hood off my head, pull the game box out from under the bed and take out the instructions.

In the table of contents I look for something that sounds like „Earning money“, and as I find a reference, I open the relevant page and read it.It explains a lot of things that have already been mentioned in the game, and it takes me a while to find the information I'm looking for. Then I read the paragraph carefully.

As if on cue, the reminder function on my cell phone rings. I have to be at the university in 20 minutes!

As quickly as I can, I take off the technical pant that I'm supposed to wear next to my skin while playing and put it on to the bed. They will be used to collect the semen and send it to the company later.

I'm not worried about the sperm becoming unusable, because the instructions say that the sperm is collected in a specially designed cartridge and automatically frozen.

If the battery does become too low, there is a light on the cartridge that warns you. In this case, it is important to charge it again before sending the cartridge in.

I put on my everyday clothes. On top of that I put on my winter jacket and, after lacing up my warm shoes, I take my backpack, which contains everything I need for today's study day, and leave the room.

When I arrive at the university, I walk across the large square.

Sophia, a fellow student, walks a few meters ahead of me, also in the direction of the lecture halls.

Last summer, she usually wore a sleeveless, bellybaring T-shirt with a mini skirt or tight-fitting jeans.

Now, in winter, she wears a winter coat that reaches down to her knees. Her long blonde hair sticks out from under a thick hood.

I fell in love with her body back in the summer and really wanted to have sex with her. But I never plucked up the courage to approach her and ask for it, so even now I walk a few meters behind her.

I think about meeting her in the game ... We could have sex there without me having to talk to her in real life.

Once in the lecture hall, Sophia looks for a seat. As usual, I sit three rows behind her so that I can look at her and try, as I have done so many times before, to pay attention to what the professor is teaching.

Despite everything, I want to complete my studies with a decent grade!

When I finally get back to my student room, I put my tech pant and data hood back on, lie down on my bed and start the game.

I enter the game where I left it. Barefoot on the cold earth and naked except for my underpants. I can see the two rows of medieval wooden houses in front of me again and the large fountain at the very back.

It seems to go on there, so I march towards the rows of houses and the fountain. Between the two rows, I take a close look at each house and notice signs at every house with different symbols on them. I see a blacksmith, a bow seller and a hairdresser. I can't interpret the other signs.

„Greetings, dear sir!“, a man approaches me at an extension to one of the houses. In his outfit, he looks like a salesman for leather or fabric clothing. However, the sword strapped around his waist leads me to believe that he must have something to do with fighting too.

„You look like you need silver coins“, he says.

I don't say anything back.

The way he emphasizes the words irritates me. It reminds me of movies from the Middle Ages.

„Are you interested in warrior training?“

Interesting! Apparently I can choose a profession here.

Warrior - why not? I can give it a try.

„Yes, I'm interested."

„So long!", is his reply as he gestures in the direction of a door.

He opens it, we both walk through and enter a meadow.

It is a small garden that seems to belong to his house. At the very back of the garden is a stand with axes and swords of various sizes and designs leaning against it.

„Now choose a weapon!", my teacher says, almost in a commanding tone.

I grab one of the swords and I am surprised by its weight. It's lighter than I expected.

He also takes a sword and stands some distance away from me.

„I will attack you now! Do your best to defend yourself!"

I strike a pose that I think will be a good way to fend off his sword. I take the sword hilt in both hands, although the hilt is actually too short for this.

However, this gives me a better feeling when holding the sword.

„Are you ready?", the teacher asks me.

„Yes“, I answer him and keep a close eye on what he’s doing now. I don’t want to be surprised by any of his movements.

He now also assumes what looks to me like a defensive pose, holds his sword protectively in front of him and moves slowly towards me.

In this way, we dance around each other, sometimes closer together, sometimes further apart. Whenever he gets dangerously close to me, I go back away nervously.

Although this is all simulated, it feels very real. What if he chops off my arm or drill through my shoulder?

Does that hurt as much as in real life? I don’t want that!

Finally, when he is close to me, he swings his sword.

I immediately drop mine, throw myself on the floor, protecting my head, squeeze my eyes tightly shut and scream.

Nothing happens ... I feel no sting, no cut. Nothing at all!

I open my eyes and relax again. The warrior teacher stands before me, amused. The hand that just held his weapon is now casually hanging down and the sword is stuck in the ground next to him.

„Well, Sir! I don't think you're fit to be a warrior!"

He laughs mockingly and walks towards the weapon rack.

As I stand up, he puts his weapon down, comes back to me and says:

„Talk to the archer teacher, you'll find him next to my house. Maybe you're better as a archer!"

After saying this, he leaves the garden and leaves me alone. I lean the sword against the weapon stand in its place and leave the garden too.

Back on the flat ground, I take a look at the houses next to the warrior teacher's house.

The one on the left appears to be unoccupied, but someone is standing in front of the one on the right. It is a man again. He is clearly wearing leather armor. Instead of a sword, like the teacher before him, he has a bow slung over his shoulder. It is a bow, as is usually found in bow-and-arrow sets, and next to it is a quiver with arrows in it.

This is probably the archer teacher.

This time, however, I seriously consider whether this should be my profession and answer this question immediately with a clear „no".

So I'll keep looking. Hopefully there will be even more professions in the game than these two.

Someone is standing next to the archer teacher's house. This time it is not a man, but a woman, and what is immediately noticeable is her clothing. Completely different from the two men before, she is wearing armor that leaves many parts of her body uncovered. The armor looks like a very skimpy leather-and-metal bikini, except for the covered arms and legs.

The leather and metal bikini looks stunning together with her slim figure and the hint of abdominal muscles and I find it hard not to look at her.

She seems to feel my gaze, because she turns towards me.

„Greetings, stranger!“, she calls to me and moves a few steps in my direction.

Now that she's getting closer, I notice her face too. It is enchantingly beautiful! It's as if someone had thought about how to make this woman look as perfect as possible. Only the pointy ears sticking out between her long silver-grey hair are unusual, but they harmonize very well with the rest of her body.

„Do you want to learn how to use magic wands?“, she asks when she reaches me, interrupting my thoughts.

Only now do I notice the long staff she holding in her hand. Like her bikini, it is beautifully decorated and a large crystal is worked into a setting at its upper end.

„Um, ... yes ...“, comes out of my mouth uncoordinatedly, as it always does when I’m talking to a beautiful woman.

She smiles at me as if we’ve known each other for a long time and hooks her arm in mine.

„Then come with me!“, she says and walks with me into the garden of her house.

There she gives me a wand that looks similar to hers but is much smaller. In my hand, it feels more like a toy than something you can use to hurt others or use magic with it.

We stand in the middle of the garden a few meters apart.

„You have to move the wand up and back to the starting position to tell him that you want to use his magic“, she says to me.

I swing my wand accordingly and still feel like I’m handling a toy.

But then something happens. The crystal begins to glow a faint blue and emits a soft buzzing sound.

„Excellent!“, says the sorceress. „With this, the wand informs you that it is now ready for your instructions.“

Now she also raises her rod slightly and lowers it again, whereupon the large crystal on it also glows blue. However, its glow is much more impressive than the glow of my staff.

„Look and learn!“, the sorceress demands.

I nod and watch her very closely:

She raises her rod again, swings it slightly backwards and then forwards in a long arc. The blue glow of the crystal changes to red and it looks as if it is burning inside.

Something burning is now actually shooting out of it, scorching the grass on the ground in front of me and then burning up.

„This is how you create a fireball!“

The sorceress makes a gesture with her hand and asks me: „Now try it yourself!“

I imitate her movement. Apparently I'm doing it right, because the color of my crystal also turns red and shortly afterwards a small fireball shoots out. It doesn't fly as far as the sorceress and burns less grass than hers, but at least it does the right thing before it burns out.

„Very good, sir!“, praises the teacher. „You must have learned how to wield a magic wand in the cradle.“

„Try this movement“, she says and shows me another way to guide the wand so that it releases wind.

„The spell is for your protection“, she explained.

„The wind should, if the magic is strong enough, keep your enemies from getting too close to you.“

I also perform this movement and produce some wind. It’s far too little to keep attackers away, but I probably just have to practice.

Proud of myself, I see at my little magic wand.

„You were able to implement all the lessons perfectly!“, says the teacher and is now standing right in front of me.

„As a reward, you will now receive your first wizard’s robe.“

She touches me with her rod, which makes my muscles feel strange, as if someone has inflated them. I also feel more muscular than before.

She touches me again with the wand and now it seems as if fabric is growing over my skin. I can watch as the fabric spreads across my chest and soon covers my whole body.

After what the sorceress has just said, a wizard’s robe apparently grows over my body, and when the magic has finished its work, I see that it is a robe like the ones I know from other fantasy games. It is tight fitting, but still comfortable to wear and I have the impression that it shows off my muscles.

My feet are now covered too. I now wear fabric shoes, which are also very comfortable.

„Finally, because of your stunning appearance and because you were able to carry out the instructions so brilliantly, you deserve another reward“, says the sorceress and puts her arms on my shoulders.

Her mouth is very close to mine now. She lovingly licks my upper lip. Surprised, I flinch a little, but then I open my mouth and welcome her tongue.

As we keep inviting each other to feel and taste our tongues and lips, we sit down on the soft grass. I let my hands slide down her naked back and back up her sides.

I feel her soft skin against my fingertips, and when I reach her metallic bikini breastplates, I try to find a mechanism to take them off. When I don’t succeed, I use my hands to penetrate the space between her breasts and the armor in front of them.

When the sorceress interrupts the game of our mouths, she opens my pants and pushes out my stiff penis. She wraps it with both hands and pampers him from all sides with her tongue. She takes him in her mouth again and again and also pleasures him with her hands. It’s a wonderful feeling, as if she’s already making love to me.

I close my eyes, lie down on the grass and enjoy.

When I open them again, she touches her metallic bikini-pant with a finger, causing them to spring open and expose her pubic area. She pushes her lower body onto my penis, which penetrates her.

I can feel her genital area contracting rhythmically. This motivates my penis and elicits a soft whisper from the sorceress.

Suddenly she moves her pelvis sometimes faster, sometimes slower, sometimes in circular movements, sometimes just back and forth. In between, she holds still for a moment until the moaning turns into an almost suppressed, sung cry.

The waves in her pubic area move over my penis and into my loins. More and more pressure builds up inside me, which is finally released in a scream. It's a long, prolonged orgasm, and the movements of the enchantress ensure that new waves keep firing up my penis via her insides until she tears open her mouth and releases the sung scream into the open world.

It takes a while before she opens her eyes and utters an unintelligible „Arwpuh ...".

Sweaty, she rolls off me and into the grass next to me.

One of my hands is still clutching her breast. I can feel the metal of the breastplate on the back of my hand and the warm, soft skin of her breast in my hand and I would love to never let go, but the sorceress regains her strength and says:

„Thank you for this wonderful ride. You were fantastic, my lord!“

With one hand she grabs my hand, which is still holding her breast, and says:

„You can now let go of my bosom ...“

I loosen the grip and slide my hand out from under the tank. She closes the metallic bikini panty with a flick of her wrist, stands up and leaves the garden.

I put the penis back in my pants and think by myself:

Did the newfound muscles get her so horny?

Or is this a reward that all new players get as soon as they clear another hurdle?

Anyway ... It was fantastic!

I leave the garden too and want to continue exploring the area when the sorceress calls me again from a distance:

„I have something else for you, stranger.“

Something else? What could that be?

I go to her and when I am close enough to understand her, she continues to speak.

„I need wood from a special tree to make more wands. You would have to travel to Kavna. Don't worry! You will be rewarded for it.“

She gives me an envelope similar to the one I received at the bar. I open it and read it:

Greetings, dear sir!

Travel to Kavna. There, in the caves of Kavna, you will find a wide grown tree. It is known among wizards as „The Tree of Magic".

Please bring me these things from this tree:
- *Part of its root (at least a little finger long)*
- *Part of a branch (at least one arm's length long)*
- *A young flower (completely preserved)*
- *One leaf (completely preserved)*

Reward:
3 silver coins, 9 bronze coins

Sincere thanks
The magic teacher from Arewa

When I read the letter, the sorceress asked me: „Do you want to accept this assignment?"

I think about it.

Silver and bronze coins ... It certainly doesn’t hurt to earn some in-game money. This will be necessary at some point in order to progress in the game.

„I accept the assignment“, I say to the sorceress. She smiles at me. „Thank you,“ she replies and returns to her original pose.

„But how do I get to Kavna?“, I ask her.

She turns to me and tells me that I can find a sign by the fountain that should help me.

Okay! Well then ...

The term „fountain“ probably refers to the fountain that can be seen at the end of the path between the two rows of houses.

So I go there. A few meters away is a large blackboard, like the ones you see at school, and on it is an extensive chalk drawing of the city „Arewa“ pictured.

That must be the name of the town I’m in. I recognize the row of houses where the warrior teacher’s house and the magic teacher’s house are located. The beach and the bar where I first entered the game and the fountain here by the table are also easy to find. But I can‘t find the town Kavna.

Maybe I could ask someone for directions? I look around ...

To my left, a man is sweeping the floor of his - what is it? A restaurant, apparently. Maybe he can help me.

I go to him and ask my question.

Unfortunately, he has no idea either, but there is obviously a carriage that passes by here every now and then, and the coachman should actually know how to get to Kavna. When I ask when the carriage will next pass by here, he points to the board with the map of the town on it.

So I go back to the plan and take another close look at it. I try to pay attention to things that I might have missed before.

After a few minutes of unsuccessful searching, I see in the corner of my eye that the guy that still cleaning his Restaurant, pointing to something below the plan. I look there.

Below the board hangs a small, elongated sign on which is written „Friday“, and below that:

„Register for the carriage:“.

Like the map of the city above, the text on the sign has also been applied with chalk and I wonder whether the game also realistically simulates things like rain. Neither the map nor the small sign are protected against it.

Well, it doesn't matter now. Apparently the coach is coming by on Friday. What day of the week is it today? I have no idea ...

So back to the restaurant floor sweeper and ask.

He no longer sweeps in front of his house. Maybe he's gone inside in the meantime. So I go into the restaurant and look for him.

I finally find him refilling some spirits at the bar and ask. He obviously doesn't want to talk to me right now, but tells me anyway: „Today is Friday."

What a coincidence, the coach is coming today.

But when, at what time? Do I have to stay by the sign and wait so that I don't miss the departure? Can the game really be programmed like this? I don't think so.

I think again about the sign under the city map and what is written there: „Sign up for the carriage:".

Where do I have to register?

For goodness sake! Is that complicated! The developers have come up with some really bad non-sense.

Who would that now? Back to the restaurant again.

The guy is already annoyed and says he doesn't know.

„Damn developers! Do they have to make it so complicated?“, I curse on the way out.

I guess I have no choice but to log out of the game and find myself back in the real world a few seconds later.

I take off the data cap and take off the safety pants. Then I put both back in the game box, sit down at my desk and start my computer.

To find the support e-mail address, I type the name of the game into the search engine, together with the word „support“, and when I have found it, I write the corresponding e-mail and send it off. Now I have to wait for a reply.

The journey to Kavna

I'm sitting in my usual chair in the lecture hall in the university building and trying to concentrate on the lecture. Unfortunately, it doesn't work very well because Sophia is sitting diagonally in front of me and my eyes keep turning to her.

Her sitting position causes one side of her T-shirt to bulge outwards and I can see the base of her breasts. Today it looks as if she's not wearing a bra again, which gives me a hint of its shape through the fabric and makes me want more ...

For over a year now, I've been trying to pluck up the courage to ask her for a date or simply ask for sex.

Over a year already!

That is how long we've been studying together here in the university.

I go to her in my imagination because I still lack the courage to actually do it.

What do I say to her?

Maybe: „Hey, want to have sex?"

Or: „Hello, I noticed you!"

Although the second might not sound bad at all, I know myself and my reactions. As soon as I stand in front of her, all that comes out of me is gibberish ...

For other men, this may only be a little embarrassing, but for me it's almost unbearable. In such cases I immediately want to run away and find a hiding place where I won't be found and stay there.

To make matters worse, I haven't been able to progress in the „Sex on Sagea" game for weeks. That's why the only sex I can have there at the moment is with the barmaids in the beach area. It's okay, but the artificial intelligence of the ladies there seems rather limited to me.

It's as if I'm always sleeping with the same woman, but she always looks different. So: new person, same movements and positions.

Back in my student room, I start the e-mail program, as I always have in the last few weeks, to see if the support team has replied.

It searches for new incoming e-mails and shows me that there is also one from the game support.

At last!

Excited, I open it and read.

It's a step-by-step guide to what I need to do to be able to travel in the carriage, and when I read the words, I can't believe my eyes ...

Who comes up with something like that? Oh, man!

I take out the game box, put on my pants and data cap, find a comfortable position in bed and press the start button.

Back in the game, I get my bearings.

I'm standing exactly where I left it last time, in front of the bar at the barmaids‘ on the beach.

My path now leads me to the high fence gate, where I step out of the property and continue towards the fountain. I want to get to the board with the map of the town on it.

When I arrive, two people are already standing there. A man in a robe similar to mine and a woman, apparently a female archer, in a matt leather suit that shows skin at the right places. Her pants look like bikini panties, consisting of a leather part that is held in place by two broad metal straps around her hips. The straps also hold the legs of her leather pants in place.

A tight top conceals large parts of her belly and chest and emphasizes her slim figure.

She wears matt leather gloves that reach over her arms and cover one shoulder.

What is striking about the woman is that her mouth and nose are also covered with something made of leather.

Is that a kind of leather scarf? And how does it give her enough air to breathe?

„Hello“, I greet the man and the woman.

„Hello“, comes back from both of them.

„Are you waiting for the carriage too?“

They both nod.

„Can’t be long now!“, says the woman, „I signed up a few minutes ago.“

She points her finger at the smaller panel under the card. There I see two „x“ painted next to the words „Register for the carriage:“. I assume these are the markings that the Support mentioned in the email. He writes in it that you have to sign up for transportation on the board using any sign.

According to what the woman said, it will take a few more minutes. Well then! Let’s wait ...

A little later, I hear the distant sound of horses trotting slowly closer, and soon afterwards I see a carriage coming towards us.

She drives slowly, very slowly, until she finally comes to a stop after a few minutes.

The man hastily opens the door and jumps in. The woman gives me a sign to get in before her, so I do.

We sit on a wooden plank, and when the carriage starts moving, feel a strong jolt. It seems to me that the horse-drawn carriage is now moving much faster than when it entered the town and approached the stop.

The roads are bumpy. We are now driving much faster than a carriage would in real life and I can feel every bump in the road. I hold on to the seat board so I don't slide off.

We drive like this for a while until a thought comes to my mind: How do I know that Kavna is on our way?

Damn, I forgot to ask the coachman about it ... What do I do now?

I ask my fellow travelers this question.

The man ignores me. The woman turns her head towards me.

„Ahh, new to the game, are you?"

Before I can answer, she leans forward with her upper body and shows me with her index finger that I should lean forward too.

As I do so, she touches my arms with her hand as if she wants to feel my muscles. Then she removes her scarf from her mouth and nose, exposing her pretty face.

„Do you want to kiss me?“

I glance uncertainly at our fellow traveler, who is staring out of the carriage window, lost in thought.

If we were alone, I would kiss her properly now, but this way I purse my lips for a peck.

„No, no! Not like that. ... Like this!“, she says, opens her mouth and penetrates mine with her tongue. I let it happen. My tongue feels hers. But not wild and full of desire, like the sorceress's a few weeks ago, but tender and exploratory, as if she wants to get to know the shape of my tongue. I gradually hear her sighing softly. Or are we both sighing?

I feel the desire to touch her hip and to feel her butt in my hand, but I don't want to do anything that might scare her away. Unlike the game-controlled characters I've met so far, I'm pretty sure this woman is a player. In other words, a real person.

The longer the kiss lasts, the greater this desire becomes and so at some point I risk it anyway.

I stroke the sides of her buttocks with my hands and, to my surprise, she seems to like it. She moves her hips in unison with my touch. This motivates me and so I move my hands closer to her bottom.

But now it's apparently too much for her, because she ends the kiss and sits up straight again.

„Mmh, you taste good!", she says and covers her mouth and nose with the leather again.

„As for your earlier question ...", she continues, „look at the place name signs! And if you want to get off, give the coachman a sign to stop."

Oh well, I think to myself. So watching out for the signs.

„But the coach goes to Kavna too, does it?", I
ask to be on the safe side.

„Yes", she says. „I'm going there myself. But if you want to go to Kavna, you have to get off at Kaverna."

Kaverna? I thought I have to go to Kavna!

I look at her questioningly.

„Kavna is a mountain in Kaverna!", she explains to
me.

Glad to have this information, I say thank you and continue looking out of the window so as not to miss the place name signs.

After a while, I actually see a sign coming towards us and when it is close enough to read it, I know that we are at least in the right place. The sign says „Kaverna“, and while I'm still thinking about how to find the Kavna Caves, the woman bangs her fist against the wall of the carriage and shouts:

„Coachman! Get out!“, whereupon the carriage stops after a few meters and she gets out.

Because I'm in the right place now and just have to find the mountain and the caves, I get out too. Maybe the woman knows how to get there.

She leaves the road immediately after getting out and crosses a field. I follow her and call out to her:

„Hey, can you please tell me how to get to Mount Kavna? I need to get to the deep caves!“

She stops abruptly and turns around to me.

„The caves? I'm heading there too. What task do you have to do?“

I take out the sorceress's letter, open it and read it to her.

„Okay! I don't know where you'll find all this stuff, but I can show you an entrance to the caves. I have work to do there too. Just follow me!“

She turns around again and continues walking. I follow behind her.

After crossing a few fields, we come to a high hill with a hole at the bottom. We walk towards it and when we get there, my companion stops.

„Here is one of the cave entrances!“

She squeezes herself into the rather small entrance and I do the same.

Finally inside, she explains to me:

„The caves go deep into the ground and branch upwards into the mountain.“

She goes further in and I follow her.

It is a fairly wide and deep cave, from which passages presumably lead to other caves, and it is well lit.

I wonder where the light comes from.

The walls, ceiling and floor are made of different types of earth and stone. All kinds of greenery grows there and thick roots keep poking through the stone.

I take a closer look around ... Is there anything here that I need?

Suddenly my companion screams. Has she injured herself? I want to run to her, but now I hear metal clashing against metal. Are those swords? Is someone attacking her?

I'm standing in front of the passage to the next cave, and if an attacker comes through, I'm practically sitting on the serving plate. So I press my back against the wall as quickly as possible so that I can't be seen immediately from the corridor and the next cave.

Another scream from her. Shortly afterwards, a pitiful sound from a man. Then silence ...

What's going on? Is she all right?

„Are you OK?“, I call out into the corridor.

„Yes, everything's fine!“, comes back from her immediately.

„You can come in! I chased him away!“

I leave the cover and enter the new section.

My companion kneels over a root sticking out of the rock and drips something from a small bottle onto it.

„So, I still need thirteen roots!“, she announces.

Then she gets up and disappears into the next passageway.

So she's also doing a job ...

Then I should probably also do my job in these caves.

I take out the sorceress's letter and read what I need again:

Part of its root (at least a little finger long)

That's a good thing! I can break off a part of the root here and take it with me. At least if it belongs to the tree of magic ... But how do I find out?

I crouch down in front of it and try to break off a part of it as a test. It turns out to be harder than I thought, the root is very robust ... But somehow I manage to tear it out of the rock and think: How do I check whether the root is from the right tree?

Is there perhaps still something in the order? Have I missed something?

I take another look at the letter.

I can't find any additional information anywhere, but the line „*Part of its root (at least a little finger long)*“ is now crossed out and there is a little check-mark next to it.

Cool! So I've got the right root. What else do I need now?

Part of a branch, a young flower and a leaf.

I now start to do the same as my companion, searching all the passages and caves.

If something looks like I could use it, I pick it or tear it off the plant. Then I check whether it was the right one, and if so, I take it with me.

My companion and I keep running always in each others path while we gather our needs. She is completely concentrated in her task and doesn't notice me.

When I have finished everything, I stop in the cave and wait for my companion to finish, but she is still very busy. I ask her if I can help her, whereupon she pauses and looks at me.

„I'm afraid that's not possible ...“ she says briefly and continues with her task.

I go back to the place in the cave where we entered the hill, sit down on a rock and wait ...

After a while, when I'm already wondering whether she might have used a different cave exit, she turns up.

„Now I've got everything! That was a lot of work. ... Have you got everything too?“

„Yep!“ is my curt reply.

She nods.

„Then let's go back to Arewa now and hand in the orders.“

„Hand in orders?“

She looks at me, puzzled.

„That means you go back to the person that gave you the job. Then you tell her that you completed it and then collect the reward.“

„Okay, I see!“

My companion sets off. I follow again.

„And why walking? Why don't we take the carriage again?“

„Because the next stop of the the carriage is in Kaverna. We have to walk about the same distance to get there as we do from here back to Arewa.“

I see! That makes sense!

On the way, she tells me a few anecdotes about her adventures in the game. I tell her something about my real life and find out that she lives in Russia and is called Aleksandra. Impressed by her perfect German, I ask where and how she learned it. She tells me that she grew up in Germany for a long time, but that her parents are fans of Russia they moved there at some point.

When we arrive in Arewa, I ask her again how it works with handing in the order. She explains it in more detail and tells me to contact her if I would like to do something with her again. Of course, I'm delighted by this offer and say „I'd love to!"

Then we say goodbye and go our separate ways, I go straight to the magic teacher. As expected, I find her waiting outside her house, just as seductive as before.

„Hello!", I say to her.

„Greetings, dear sir! How can I help you?"

I take out the letter with the description of the order, in which all the points are now clearly crossed out and marked with a green checkmark, and give it to her.

„I have completed the task and would like to have the reward."

She reads through the letter and smiles.

„Excellent! Please put everything on the table here." She points to a table in front of her house.

„Then talk to me again and you'll receive your reward."

She ends the conversation and returns to her original pose.

So I put everything on the table and talk to her again. She hands out a few coins to me, which I immediately stow away in my chest.

Next, I would like to know what the money can buy, but not now. I should return to the real world and continue with the lecture preparations for the next study day. So I say the words to log out and a few moments later I'm lying in my bed.